nice and cozy

by Bijou Le Tord

Four Winds Press
New York

LIBRARY OF CONGRESS CATALOGING IN PUBLICATION DATA

Le Tord, Bijou.
  Nice and cozy.
  SUMMARY: Tommy the pig wants to fly before he finds
happiness with Sweet Martha.
  [1. Pigs—Fiction. 2. Flight—Fiction]
I. Title.
PZ7.L568Ni [E]   80-11376   ISBN 0-590-07668-X

PUBLISHED BY FOUR WINDS PRESS
A DIVISION OF SCHOLASTIC MAGAZINES, INC., NEW YORK, N.Y.
COPYRIGHT ©1980 BY BIJOU LE TORD
ALL RIGHTS RESERVED
PRINTED IN THE UNITED STATES OF AMERICA
LIBRARY OF CONGRESS CATALOG CARD NUMBER: 80-11376
1 2 3 4 5 84 83 82 81 80

To Joan

Over the blue mountains
there is a piggy.
His name is Tommy.
wee wee wee

There is also another piggy.

Her name is Sweet Martha.

She is pretty as could be.

wee wee wee

"O Sweet Martha," said Tommy,
"I want to fly in the sky.
Then I'll marry you."
wee wee wee

So he launched his boat
and pulled and swung the oars,
but he couldn't fly.
wee wee wee

He paddled with water wings!
and stirred on the pond,
but he couldn't fly.
wee wee wee

"Tommy!" said Sweet Martha.
"You can't fly.
Stay out of the sky."
wee wee wee

So he felt blue inside
and he felt blue outside
and he cried.

wee wee wee

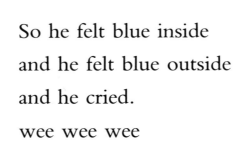

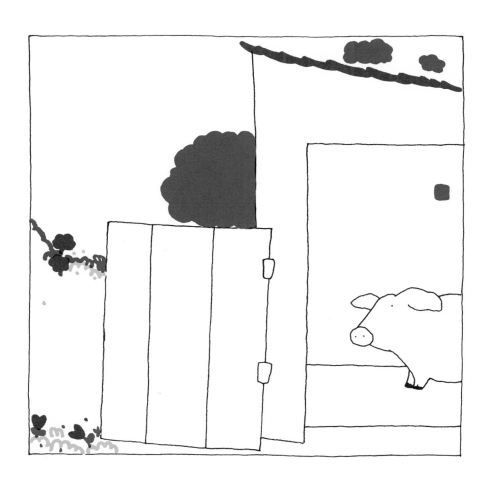

So by night he took his sleigh
and said good-bye
and flew far across the sky.
wee wee wee

He flew and flew
till the stars
turned into flowers.
wee wee wee

The rain brought him down.
"Oh! my Tommy," said Sweet Martha
from under the tree.
wee wee wee

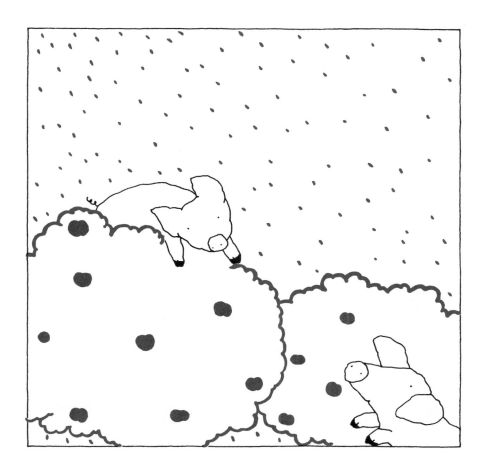

"O Martha, Sweet Martha,
I flew all night for you.
Will you marry me?"
wee wee wee

"I will, I will," said Martha,
"with flowers everywhere.
    And we will be nice and cozy."
wee wee wee

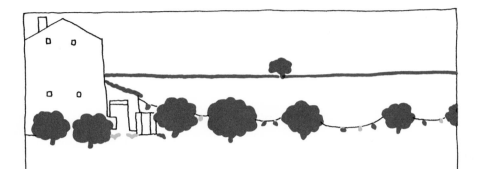

It was a pretty wedding.
Sweet Martha said, "I do, I do,"
and Tommy said, "I love you!"
wee wee wee

Together they watched the sky
and Sweet Martha said,
"One day you and I will fly."
Wee Wee Wee Wee Wee